Night of the Ninth Dragon

Magic Tree House® Books

#1: Dinosaurs Before Dark
#2: The Knight at Dawn
#3: Mummies in the Morning
#4: Pirates Past Noon
#5: Night of the Ninjas
#6: Afternoon on the Amazon
#7: Sunset of the Sabertooth
#8: Midnight on the Moon
#9: Dolphins at Daybreak
#10: Ghost Town at Sundown
#11: Lions at Lunchtime
#12: Polar Bears Past Bedtime
#13: Vacation Under the Volcano
#14: Day of the Dragon King
#15: Viking Ships at Sunrise
#16: Hour of the Olympics
#17: Tonight on the *Titanic*
#18: Buffalo Before Breakfast
#19: Tigers at Twilight
#20: Dingoes at Dinnertime
#21: Civil War on Sunday
#22: Revolutionary War on Wednesday
#23: Twister on Tuesday
#24: Earthquake in the Early Morning
#25: Stage Fright on a Summer Night
#26: Good Morning, Gorillas
#27: Thanksgiving on Thursday
#28: High Tide in Hawaii

Merlin Missions

#29: Christmas in Camelot
#30: Haunted Castle on Hallows Eve
#31: Summer of the Sea Serpent
#32: Winter of the Ice Wizard
#33: Carnival at Candlelight
#34: Season of the Sandstorms
#35: Night of the New Magicians
#36: Blizzard of the Blue Moon
#37: Dragon of the Red Dawn
#38: Monday with a Mad Genius
#39: Dark Day in the Deep Sea
#40: Eve of the Emperor Penguin
#41: Moonlight on the Magic Flute
#42: A Good Night for Ghosts
#43: Leprechaun in Late Winter
#44: A Ghost Tale for Christmas Time
#45: A Crazy Day with Cobras
#46: Dogs in the Dead of Night
#47: Abe Lincoln at Last!
#48: A Perfect Time for Pandas

#49: Stallion by Starlight
#50: Hurry Up, Houdini!
#51: High Time for Heroes
#52: Soccer on Sunday
#53: Shadow of the Shark
#54: Balto of the Blue Dawn

Super Editions

Danger in the Darkest Hour

Magic Tree House® Fact Trackers

Dinosaurs
Knights and Castles
Mummies and Pyramids
Pirates
Rain Forests
Space
Titanic
Twisters and Other Terrible Storms
Dolphins and Sharks
Ancient Greece and the Olympics
American Revolution
Sabertooths and the Ice Age
Pilgrims
Ancient Rome and Pompeii
Tsunamis and Other Natural Disasters
Polar Bears and the Arctic
Sea Monsters
Penguins and Antarctica
Leonardo da Vinci
Ghosts
Leprechauns and Irish Folklore
Rags and Riches: Kids in the Time of Charles Dickens
Snakes and Other Reptiles
Dog Heroes
Abraham Lincoln
Pandas and Other Endangered Species
Horse Heroes
Heroes for All Times
Soccer
Ninjas and Samurai
China: Land of the Emperor's Great Wall
Sharks and Other Predators
Vikings
Dogsledding and Extreme Sports
NEW! Dragons and Mythical Creatures

More Magic Tree House®

Games and Puzzles from the Tree House
Magic Tricks from the Tree House
My Magic Tree House Journal
Magic Tree House Survival Guide
Animal Games and Puzzles

MAGIC TREE HOUSE® #55
A MERLIN MISSION

Night of the Ninth Dragon

by Mary Pope Osborne

illustrated by Sal Murdocca

A STEPPING STONE BOOK™

Random House 🏠 New York

Visit us on the Web!
SteppingStonesBooks.com
randomhousekids.com
MagicTreeHouse.com

Educators and librarians, for a variety of teaching tools, visit us at
RHTeachersLibrarians.com

Library of Congress Cataloging-in-Publication Data is available upon request.

ISBN 978-0-553-51089-8 (trade) — ISBN 978-0-553-51090-4 (lib. bdg.)—
ISBN 978-0-553-51091-1 (ebook)

Printed in the United States of America

10 9 8 7 6 5 4 3 2

This book has been officially leveled by using the F&P Text Level Gradient™ Leveling System.

For our dear friend
Dharani Burnham

CONTENTS

Prologue 1

1. That's It? 3

2. Hail, Your Majesty! 12

3. Dragons Everywhere 24

4. Just Us 34

5. Cafelle and Kee 46

6. Riddle of the Forest 57

7. Run for Your Lives! 68

8. Munith Mor 81

9. Fire Dragon 91

10. All Good 102

11. Back to the Garden 114

Excerpt from *Dragons and Mythical Creatures* 123

Prologue

One summer day in Frog Creek, Pennsylvania, a mysterious tree house appeared in the woods. It was filled with books. A boy named Jack and his sister, Annie, found the tree house and soon discovered that it was magic. They could go to any time and place in history just by pointing to a picture in one of the books. While they were gone, no time at all passed back in Frog Creek.

Jack and Annie eventually found out that the tree house belonged to Morgan le Fay, a magical librarian from the legendary realm of Camelot. They have since traveled on many adventures in the magic tree house and completed many missions for both Morgan le Fay and her friend Merlin the magician. Teddy and Kathleen, two young enchanters from Camelot, have sometimes helped Jack and Annie in both big and small ways.

Jack and Annie are about to find out what their next magic tree house mission will be!

CHAPTER ONE
That's It?

The day was cloudy and windy. Jack was sitting on the front porch, using a yellow marker to highlight a book called *Caring for Your New Puppy*.

"Fetch, Oki!" Annie shouted, throwing a ball across their yard.

Yip, yip! A scruffy black-and-white puppy raced after the ball and caught it in his mouth. "Bring it back!" Annie called. But Oki dashed away from her instead.

"He never does what you say," Jack said with a laugh.

"Yes, he does," said Annie. "He fetched! He just decided not to bring it back." She ran after Oki and wrestled the ball away from him. "Ready to go to the dog park now?" she called to Jack.

"Yep." Jack highlighted a paragraph about puppy dental care. Then he closed the book and dropped it into his pack along with his yellow marker. "All set."

"Did you pack supplies?" said Annie.

"Just his leash and water bowl," said Jack. "And some puppy treats." He pulled the leash out of his pack.

"Wait. Let's see if he'll walk with us on his own," said Annie.

"If I know him, he'll take off," said Jack.

"Come on, give him a chance. I've been working with him," said Annie. "Watch. Oki! Come!" The little dog ran to Jack and Annie.

"See?" said Annie as they started down the sidewalk.

"Do you really think he'll stay with us?" said Jack, putting the leash back in his pack.

"Sure," said Annie.

"Hey, do you have any money?" Jack asked.

"What for?" said Annie.

"I thought we could stop at the pet store," said Jack. "We need to get him a dog toothbrush and toothpaste. I was just reading that canine tooth care is very important. You have to—" Before Jack could finish, Oki yipped and dashed away down the sidewalk.

"Oki, wait! Oki!" shouted Annie. "Stay!"

But the puppy kept running. He crossed the street, bounded over the curb, and disappeared into the Frog Creek woods.

"I knew it!" Jack said.

"Oki!" Annie shouted. She and Jack raced into the woods after the puppy. Tree branches were waving in the wind. Dry autumn leaves shook and rustled.

"Oki!" yelled Jack.

"You were right!" wailed Annie. "We should have put him on the leash!"

"Don't worry, we'll find him," said Jack.

"Oki!" they called. "Oki!"

Yip, yip!

"Did you hear that?" said Jack.

"Yes!" Annie and Jack took off running between the trees. They followed the yipping sounds—until they found the puppy at the base of a giant oak tree.

The magic tree house was nestled high in the treetop. The rope ladder was swaying from side to side.

"Good boy, Oki!" Annie said. She picked up the puppy and giggled as he licked her face. "How did you know it was back?"

"Teddy?" Jack called, looking up at the tree house. "Teddy?"

There was no answer, and no one looked down from the window.

"Let's climb up," said Annie. "There must be a message inside."

Yip? Yip?

"Yes, you're coming with us!" Annie said to Oki. "Here, get in Jack's bag." Jack took off his backpack, and Annie lowered the puppy inside. "Is that going to be too heavy?"

"No, he doesn't weigh much," said Jack, pulling on the pack. "Let's go, buddy." Jack carried Oki up the rope ladder, and Annie followed.

When they had all climbed into the tree house, Jack took off his pack and set it on the floor. Oki scampered out and began sniffing every corner.

"I don't see anything here," said Annie, looking around.

"Me neither," said Jack. There was no message from Merlin, no book from Morgan. "There's nothing here to tell us what to do."

Yip, yip, yip! Oki was looking out the window, barking at the woods.

Jack looked up and saw a scrap of paper floating on the wind. "Hey, is that our note?" he said.

"It must have blown out of the window!" said Annie. "I'll get it." She hurried back down the rope ladder. Oki kept barking as Annie chased after the paper and finally snatched it from the ground.

Annie read the note to herself and smiled.

Annie read the note to herself.

"What does it say?" Jack called.

"Good news!" said Annie.

"What? What is it?" said Jack.

"See for yourself!" said Annie. She scrambled back up the ladder and handed Jack the scrap of paper. "Our favorite place to visit."

Jack looked at the old-fashioned handwriting:

Dear Jack and Annie,
    Please come to Camelot.

"That's it?" said Jack.

"It's good news, right?" said Annie.

"Yeah, but it doesn't look like Merlin or Morgan's handwriting, or Teddy's. . . . I don't understand. Who wrote this? And why?" said Jack.

"It doesn't matter," said Annie. "It's an invitation to Camelot! I love visiting Camelot, don't you?"

"Of course," said Jack. They had visited the kingdom many times. He loved its orchards and the Great Hall and Morgan's magnificent library. Most of all, he loved their friends in Camelot. "But something's weird."

"Don't worry, Jack. Let's just go," said Annie. "Get ready, Oki!" She pointed at the word *Camelot* on the note. "I wish we could go *there!*"

Yip! Yip!

Jack grabbed Oki and held him tightly.

The wind blew harder.

The tree house started to spin.

It spun faster and faster.

Then everything was still.

Absolutely still.

CHAPTER TWO

Hail, Your Majesty!

The tree house was dark with shadows.

Yip!

Jack clutched Oki. He and the puppy both shivered in the damp, chilly air.

"Hey, our clothes didn't change," said Annie. She and Jack were still wearing their jeans, T-shirts, and sneakers.

"Right . . . ," said Jack.

"Maybe the person who invited us didn't know how to magically change our clothes," said Annie.

"Who *is* that person?" said Jack. He looked out

the window with Annie and Oki. "And where did we land, exactly?"

The tree house was in a forest of ancient-looking oak trees with gnarled roots and sprawling branches. The shadowy woodland was eerily quiet. No birds sang. No squirrels scurried over the ground.

"Are we sure this is Camelot?" asked Jack. "I wish we had a book to give us information."

"Let's go down and get information firsthand," said Annie.

"Okay," said Jack. He picked up Oki and put him inside his backpack. Then he pulled on the pack and followed Annie down the rope ladder to the forest floor.

"So . . . which way?" Jack asked, looking around at the thick, towering oaks. Here and there, a shaft of sunlight shot through the treetops.

Oki sniffed the air and barked excitedly.

"He wants to lead us somewhere," said Annie.

"Okay, but let's put him on the leash this time," said Jack. Annie lifted the puppy and the leash out of his pack. But before she could fasten the leash to Oki's collar, the puppy jumped from her arms and dashed off.

"Oki! Come back!" said Jack.

"Stop!" cried Annie.

"Oh, brother, not again!" said Jack, breaking into a run. "Oki!"

"Oki, stop!" Annie yelled.

Racing through the woods, Jack and Annie chased Oki around one huge tree and then another. They chased him through pools of light and shade, and over fallen leaves, twigs, and acorns, until the puppy dashed from the dappled dark into a bright wheat field.

"Gotcha!" Annie said, grabbing Oki.

"You've got to stick with us, buddy," said Jack as Annie attached the leash to the puppy's collar.

"Where are we now?" said Annie.

Tall yellow stalks of wheat blocked the view of the land beyond the field. All Jack could see was a faraway mountain range.

"I don't know. Let's keep going," said Jack.

With Oki pulling on his leash, Jack and Annie began pushing their way through the wheat. Morning sunlight shimmered on the tasseled stalks as they swayed in the wind.

"Oh, wow, look over there!" said Annie, pointing. Beyond the wheat, red flags waved from cone-shaped towers. Dragons decorated the flags. "King Arthur's castle!"

"Yes!" said Jack. He and Annie and Oki pushed through the stalks until they came to an open field where cut grass was piled into haystacks.

"Yay!" said Annie. "Let's go, Oki!" The puppy pulled on his leash, and they all started running across the field toward the outer wall of the castle. When they drew close, a trumpet sounded. A guard appeared between two turrets.

The guard aimed a crossbow at them.

"Annie, stop!" Jack yelled.

Oki barked wildly. Annie scooped him into her arms. "We come in peace!" she called to the guard.

"We have an invitation!" Jack shouted.

The guard scowled and kept his crossbow aimed directly at them.

"Jack! Annie!" someone called. A golden-haired woman in a green cape was hurrying through the gate in the outer wall. As she ran toward Jack and Annie, the guard slowly lowered his weapon.

"Queen Guinevere!" said Jack.

"Oh, wow!" said Annie.

"Hello! Hello!" Guinevere said when she reached Jack and Annie.

"Hail, Your Majesty!" said Jack, bowing.

"Hail, Your Majesty!" said Annie as Oki tried to wriggle out of her arms. "This is Oki, our new puppy."

"Hello, Oki." Though she smiled, Guinevere looked worried. Her golden hair was tangled, and her long gown was torn. "I am very glad to see all three of you," she said.

"Did you send the tree house for us, Your Majesty?" said Annie.

"Yes. Long ago, Morgan explained its magic to

me," said the queen. "She told me how to send for you if I ever needed your help."

"So . . . does that mean you need our help now?" said Jack.

"I will explain everything," said Guinevere. "But it is not safe outside our castle walls. Come." She beckoned for Jack and Annie to follow her back toward the gate.

Not safe? Why? Jack wondered as he and Annie hurried after the queen.

Guinevere led them through the arched gateway. In the outer yard, Jack saw no sign of knights or servants—and no plowmen or stonecutters or carpenters working on the grounds.

"Excuse me, Your Majesty, but are Merlin and Morgan here?" asked Annie. "And Teddy and Kathleen?"

"No, they left a fortnight ago," said Guinevere. "Only a small number of us are here in Camelot." She waved at a guard beside the gate in the inner wall, and he raised the iron grid that sealed off the main entrance of the castle.

"*Queen Guinevere!*" said Jack.

Jack and Annie followed the queen across a wide courtyard. As Jack looked around, he saw that the stables and forge seemed to be empty. No grooms or blacksmiths were at work. "Where is everyone, Your Majesty?" he asked.

"Ten days ago, enemy invaders came ashore in the distant east, and the king and his knights set out to defend the kingdom and push them back," the queen said. "After anxious days with no news of the battle, we received word that several bands of the invaders had slipped past the king's army and were heading toward Camelot. Before they arrived to plunder the castle, I led everyone who was still here to a hill fort hidden in the west. Yesterday I returned with only a few guards."

"Why did you come back?" Annie asked.

The queen sighed. Jack thought she looked as if she might cry. But then she steadied herself and spoke in a strong voice. "Because at the fort, I received terrible news."

"What news, Your Majesty?" asked Jack.

"I will explain," said the queen. "But first I must

take you to a secret place." Guinevere led them into the Great Hall, the main room of the palace. Beneath the vaulted ceiling, tables and benches were overturned. Broken earthenware platters and moldy crusts of bread littered the floor. Tapestries had been torn from the walls.

Jack remembered what the Great Hall had been like when he and Annie had attended a celebration there: warm, bright, and filled with music. "What happened?" he asked the queen.

"The invaders were looking for gold," she said. "They stole gold candlesticks and goblets from the chapel, and gold plates and bowls from the hall." The queen led Jack and Annie from the chilly hall into the castle kitchen and pantry. There was no clatter of cooks or scullions at work in the kitchen. No fire burned in the huge stone hearth. The wind whistled through the open windows. A rat scurried across the floor.

"Whoa," said Annie, stepping out of the way. Oki barked and squirmed in her arms.

Without even glancing at the rat, Guinevere

led them out of the kitchen, across an inner court-yard, and up a dark stairway.

"Were Merlin and Morgan scared, too?" asked Jack, climbing after the queen. "Is that why they left?"

"Oh, no, Merlin and Morgan left with Teddy and Kathleen before word came of the invaders," Guinevere said. "I believe they know nothing about what has happened to Camelot."

"Can you send a message to them, Your Majesty?" asked Annie.

"I am afraid that is impossible," the queen said. She took a torch from the wall and hurried down a narrow passageway. Jack and Annie followed her to a heavy wooden door at the end. The queen opened the door and led them into a torch-lit room.

Inhaling the sweet, woodsy smell of books, Jack recognized the room at once. "Morgan's library!" he murmured. Shelves covered the walls from floor to ceiling. The shelves were filled with books from all times and places.

"Fortunately, the thieves were not interested

in books," said the queen. "They did not steal a single one."

"Good, I'm glad," said Jack. Books were more valuable to him than gold.

"Excuse me, Your Majesty," said Annie, "but where did Morgan and Merlin go? And Teddy and Kathleen? And why can't you send word to them?"

"I'll explain in a moment," said the queen. She crossed the room and opened another heavy wooden door. Damp, fragrant air rushed in from a lush garden surrounded by tall stone walls.

"The answers to all your questions are here," said Queen Guinevere, "in Morgan le Fay's secret garden."

CHAPTER THREE
Dragons Everywhere

"**O**h, wow . . . a secret garden," whispered Annie. She put Oki down and unhooked his leash, and the puppy dashed into the lush greenery.

Guinevere led Jack and Annie through the doorway and into the walled garden. As they followed her down a stone path, they passed tangles of cream-colored lilies, butter-yellow daffodils, blue periwinkles, and pale-pink roses.

"From her plants, Morgan makes inks and paints for the books of our scribes," explained

Guinevere, "and dyes for the wool of the castle weavers."

"Cool," said Annie.

Guinevere pointed to raised earth beds in the center of the garden. "She grows flowers and herbs for healing everyday illnesses and injuries," she said.

"Like what?" asked Jack.

"Nettles for a cold," said Guinevere, "and mint for headaches." She pointed to a fishpond surrounded by yellow-green grasses and white flowers. "Lemongrass for fever, and yarrow to stop bleeding."

Jack shivered. The air felt tingly and alive. Why did he imagine they were being watched? Did he hear breathing? Whispering? The flutter of wings? Or was it just the wind blowing through the garden?

Oki started barking. He bounced up and down, yelping at something in the shrubbery. When Jack and Annie hurried to him, they found a small bronze statue of a dragon.

Jack laughed. "It's not a real dragon, Oki," he said. "It's just a statue."

Annie started to pick up the puppy. But Oki dashed to a patch of pink roses and barked again. Jack and Annie followed him and found a statue carved from pink granite. "Another dragon!" said Annie.

Oki kept bounding around the garden, yelping at more and more hidden dragon statues: a clay dragon tucked behind clay pots, an emerald dragon hidden among the ivy, a marble dragon between white stones, a silver dragon in tall silvery grass, a glass dragon and a dragon made from seashells in the shadows of the rock wall.

"Dragons everywhere!" said Jack.

Annie picked up the puppy and tried to calm him. "Don't worry, Oki," she said, "they're just garden decorations."

"No," the queen said. "These dragons are far more than garden decorations." She looked very serious. "Perhaps you have heard of King Arthur's father, Uther Pendragon?"

"I've read about him," said Jack. "Doesn't *Pendragon* mean 'Chief Dragon'?"

The queen nodded. "Indeed, it does," she said. "The emblem on King Uther's flag and shield was a dragon. And now a dragon adorns Arthur's flag and shield as well. The dragon is the symbol of the ruler of Camelot."

"Got it," said Annie.

"Before he died, Uther Pendragon ordered his craftsmen to create nine dragon statues. Each statue was to be made from a different material," said the queen.

"And those statues are the ones here in the garden?" said Jack.

"Yes," said the queen. "Merlin placed a spell on each of them. As long as the dragons are here in Morgan's garden, the kingdom's enchanters can unlock the portals to any of the nine mythical realms of Camelot."

"Wow," said Annie.

"What are the nine mythical realms?" asked Jack. "We've never heard of them."

"*Another dragon!*" said Annie.

"They are lands that cannot be traveled to directly from mortal worlds," said the queen. "And actually, you *do* know about some of them. With Merlin's help, you have made journeys to four of the mythical realms." She pointed to the silver dragon in the grass. "That dragon opens the portal to the realm of Timeless Treasures. I believe Merlin sent you there one Christmas."

"He did," said Annie. "That was our mission to find the Water of Memory and Imagination."

"And the marble dragon opens the portal to the Land-Behind-the-Clouds," said Guinevere.

"Where we met the Ice Wizard!" said Jack.

"The bronze dragon is the gateway to the realm of the Raven King," said the queen. "And the seashell statue to the realm of the Sea Serpent."

"Where we changed into seals," said Annie.

"And met Kathleen," said Jack.

"There are five realms you have not visited," said the queen. "Each of the other dragons unlocks a portal to one of them. But the most important dragon is the gold dragon, for it unlocks the portal to the most magical realm of all: the Isle of Avalon. And that is where Morgan and Merlin and Teddy and Kathleen are right now. A fortnight ago, they journeyed to Avalon for a respite."

"What's a respite?" asked Annie.

"It's like a vacation, right?" said Jack.

"Yes, but in this case, a vacation with a bit of magic," said the queen. "Morgan and Merlin go to Avalon to rest and renew themselves. There is a vast garden there, filled with the ancient secrets of healing. It is the only place where Morgan can grow plants that mend *all* wounds."

"Cool," said Annie.

"So when will they come back to Camelot?" asked Jack.

The queen sighed. "The ninth statue—the gold dragon—occupies the most important place in the garden," she said. "There, surrounded by those rosebushes." She pointed toward clusters of bright yellow roses in the far corner of the garden.

Jack and Annie hurried over to the rosebushes. But there was no dragon. They looked back at Guinevere. "Um . . . I don't see a dragon here," said Jack.

"No," said the queen. "That is because the ninth dragon has been stolen."

"Oh, no!" said Annie.

"When the invaders plundered the castle, they found their way into this garden," said the queen. "Since they were after gold, the theft of the gold dragon was likely a simple act of greed. But when they took it from its place in the garden, the portal to Avalon closed. Without the ninth dragon, Merlin, Morgan, Teddy, and Kathleen are locked out of Camelot forever."

"Forever?" breathed Jack.

"Yes," said Guinevere. "Avalon is where they are, and Avalon is where they will remain—unless we find the ninth dragon."

"We have to find it," said Annie. "We have to help them all get back!"

"Yes," said the queen. "And there is another reason to find the gold statue. I told you that I returned to the castle yesterday after I received terrible news. A messenger came from the east to tell me that King Arthur had been mortally wounded."

"*Mortally* wounded? What does that mean?" Annie asked.

Oki whined as if he understood.

Guinevere took a deep breath. "An arrow pierced the king's armor and plunged deep into his chest, close to his heart. If King Arthur does not journey to Avalon soon, he will die."

CHAPTER FOUR

Just Us

Jack gasped. He couldn't believe it.

"Oh, no," said Annie.

"Yes. Right now we have a small supply of heal-ing water from Avalon that is keeping Arthur alive," said Guinevere. "But it will not last much longer."

"What can we do?" said Jack.

"Your courage and intelligence are legendary in Camelot," said the queen. "And that is why I sent for you. Will you help me find the gold dragon so the king can journey to Avalon, where Morgan can save his life?"

"Yes!" said Annie and Jack.

"Thank you," said the queen. "He awaits us now."

"You mean King Arthur is *here*?" asked Annie.

"Yes. Sir Tristan and Sir Lamorak brought him back to Camelot two nights ago," said Guinevere. "Let us go now and see the king."

Oki scampered ahead with the queen as she led the way back through the library and down the passageway to the staircase. When they reached the inner courtyard of the castle, they crossed the cobblestones to a small private chapel. Jack picked up Oki, and the queen tapped on the chapel's door. The door slowly opened.

A bearded knight stared at Jack and Annie with dark, tired eyes. He held an iron lance. Another battle-worn knight stepped from the shadows.

When Oki growled at the two knights, Jack held him tighter. "Quiet," he whispered.

"Sir Lamorak, Sir Tristan, Jack and Annie have arrived," the queen said. "It is time to prepare."

Without a word, the two knights bowed to the queen, then strode across the courtyard.

Guinevere motioned for Jack and Annie to step inside the candlelit chapel.

"Thank you for coming, my friends," a man said in a low, hoarse voice. King Arthur was sitting in a carved wooden chair beneath a stained-glass window. In the flickering candlelight, the king's rugged, handsome face was very pale.

Yip! Oki leapt out of Jack's arms and dashed toward King Arthur.

"Oki, stay!" said Annie. Before she could grab him, the puppy jumped into the king's lap.

"What—what is this?" Arthur stammered. But when the puppy licked his face, the king smiled. "Well! Greetings, little one," he said. Then he looked up at Jack and Annie. His eyes were clouded with pain.

"Hail, Your Majesty," said Jack, bowing.

"Hail, Your Majesty," echoed Annie, bowing also. "We're so sorry to hear you were wounded."

"No talk ... of that," the king said, struggling to breathe. "I ... will ... prevail."

The queen stepped forward. "Arthur, rest," she said. "I will tell them our plan."

"No . . . I must explain," said the king. He took a deep breath, as if gathering his strength. Then, trembling, he leaned forward. "Deep in the forest lives an old woman . . . a seer who has a kind heart and the gift of prophecy . . . an old friend . . . my nursemaid long ago. . . . Her name is Cafelle. . . . She can help us find the gold dragon."

"That sounds good, Your Majesty," said Annie.

"Yes . . . yes . . . ," the king said. "The tree leaves speak to her . . . in the wind. Do . . . you . . . understand?"

"Yes, Your Majesty," said Annie.

Jack nodded, but he was a little worried that the king might have lost his mind.

Guinevere placed a hand on her husband's shoulder. "When Arthur was a boy, Cafelle told him that the wind speaks to her through the rustling of leaves. In her trances, she listens to the trees, then shares her prophecies in the form of riddles."

"That is why we sent . . . for you," said King Arthur.

"We know that you are particularly brilliant at solving riddles," said Guinevere. "If you can solve the riddle of Cafelle's prophecy, we can find the gold dragon."

"We'll do our best, Your Majesty," said Annie.

"Uh, sure," said Jack, nodding. "We'll do our best, Your Majesty."

"Good," said the queen. "Sir Tristan and Sir Lamorak are preparing for our departure."

"Cool," said Jack. He was glad the knights were traveling with them. Hopefully, they could come up with a better plan.

"Then let us go," said the king.

"No, not you, my lord," Queen Guinevere said. "You should rest here and wait for us to return with the dragon."

"But—I . . . I must go . . . ," said the king.

"I fear you should not," said Guinevere. "I will tell Cafelle—"

"No, I must go," the king repeated. "She will share her prophecies only with me."

The queen took a deep breath. "Then so be it," she said. She looked at Jack and Annie. "Please help the king rise."

Jack and Annie stepped over to the wounded king. They held his arms as he stood up from the carved wooden chair.

"Thank you. Let us go forth," said the king.

Oki scampered ahead as Jack and Annie helped Arthur out of the chapel. Then the queen slowly led them all across the courtyard toward the gatehouse.

A rumbling sound came from the stables. Jack turned to see Sir Tristan and Sir Lamorak driving a wooden hay cart across the courtyard. A pair of oxen pulled the four-wheeled cart as it wobbled over the cobblestones.

Oki rushed forward and barked at the oxen. Annie hurried after the puppy and grabbed him.

"This is our carriage," said the queen. "No one will suspect the king is riding in a hay cart."

"Let us go forth," said the king.

Jack was glad to see the two knights again. But he wondered how such a small, rickety cart could carry all six people. Would he and Annie be walking?

The oxen came to a halt, and the knights climbed down from the drivers' bench. Sir Lamorak grabbed tattered cloaks from the back of the cart and handed them to Arthur and Guinevere.

The queen helped the king pull on his disguise, then traded her green velvet cape for a patched gray cloak with a hood to hide her golden hair.

"Don *your* disguises now," she said to Jack and Annie.

Sir Tristan handed Jack and Annie two more ragged cloaks. "Thank you," said Jack. He and Annie pulled the cloaks on over their clothes.

The two knights helped the king and queen climb onto sheepskins spread over the hay. Sir Tristan handed a leather water flask to Guinevere. Then the knights stepped away.

Oki barked and squirmed in Annie's arms as if he was eager to ride in the hay cart, too. "Should he stay in the back with us?" the queen asked Jack and Annie. "Or sit with you while you drive the cart?"

Drive the cart? Won't the knights be driving the cart? Jack wondered.

"Do you really want Jack and me to drive, Your Majesty?" Annie asked.

"Yes, of course," said the queen.

"Cool. Then Oki should ride with you," said Annie. She placed the puppy in the back of the cart.

King Arthur was lying in the hay with his eyes closed. "Take care of him, Oki," whispered Annie.

The puppy scrambled over to the king and snuggled against him.

"Okay, let's go," said Jack.

He and Annie climbed up to the drivers' bench. As Annie picked up the reins, Jack looked at Sir Tristan and Sir Lamorak standing near the gatehouse. *The knights must be planning to ride horses alongside the cart,* he thought.

"Hike!" Annie shouted, using a command

they'd learned from Alaskan dogsledders.

"Wait, wait," said Jack. He looked back at the queen. "Should we wait for Sir Tristan and Sir Lamorak to get their horses, Your Majesty?"

"No, Jack. We will be traveling alone," said Guinevere. "If we come across the enemy, they must believe we are a simple family—a poor farm couple traveling with our two children."

"Sounds good," said Annie. Then she called out to the oxen again. "Hike!"

It's just us? Jack thought. *Just us?*

The oxen took a few steps forward. Their neck yoke was hitched to a wooden pole attached to the front of the cart. As they lumbered over the stones of the courtyard, the cart wobbled along behind them.

Sir Tristan raised the iron gate that sealed off the main entrance to the castle.

As the oxen headed across the outer courtyard, Annie waved to the two knights, who silently watched them leave. "See you later!" she called.

The knights each raised a hand in farewell.

"Here we go!" said Annie.

"Here we go," Jack repeated softly. "Just us." And the hay cart clattered through the gateway, leaving the castle of Camelot behind.

CHAPTER FIVE

Cafelle and Kee

"Westward, toward the mountains," said Queen Guinevere. She was sitting next to the sleeping king, with her hand resting on his chest. "Cafelle lives not far from here, where the wood borders the heath."

"Got it," said Annie. "Haw!" she called to the oxen, using the sled dog command for "Turn left!"

The heavy animals moved slowly toward the distant cloud-covered mountains. A cool, moist wind rippled through the wild grasses on either side of the rutted road.

"Where are the invaders now, Your Majesty?" asked Jack, rocking from side to side on the drivers' bench.

"We hope that our army is defeating them in the east," said the queen. "But small bands may still be roaming the kingdom, like packs of wolves."

"Like packs of wolves?" said Jack. His eyes darted around the countryside, looking for bands of invaders.

The hills and fields were covered with shadows of clouds scudding across the sun. The shadows swept over abandoned huts and farmlands with charred trees and blackened fields.

"What happened here, Your Majesty?" Annie asked. "Did the wolf packs of invaders burn everything?"

"No, the fires were set by those who live here," answered the queen. "Rumors of the enemy caused farmers to abandon their crops and hide in the hills. Before they fled, some burned their timber, barley, and flax to keep them from the invaders."

"When will everyone come back?" asked Jack.

"When they know their king has returned," the queen said. "Until then, no one will have the courage."

So everything depends on King Arthur, Jack thought, *which means everything depends on us.*

As the oxen pulled the cart toward the wooded hills and plains at the base of the mountains, the bright air grew colder and the wind stronger. The lonely road grew wilder, until it was no more than a weedy path, overgrown with thistles and brambles.

"Stop here," Guinevere said finally.

"Whoa!" said Annie.

The oxen stopped moving, and the cart jolted to a halt.

Guinevere gently shook her husband's shoulder. "Wake, my lord," she said. "Wake up."

"Yes?" the king said, lifting his head.

"We are near Cafelle's," said Guinevere. "We must walk a short way now."

Arthur sat up and looked around. Then he ran

his fingers through his hair. "Yes," he said faintly. "We must walk from here."

"First, drink this," said the queen, lifting the flask to the king's lips. Jack wondered how much of the healing water from Avalon was left. He hoped they had enough for the whole journey.

Annie climbed down from the cart bench and grabbed Oki. After Arthur drank from the flask, Guinevere helped him out of the back of the cart. King Arthur took the queen's arm, and the two of them started walking slowly down a path.

As Jack and Annie followed the royal couple through the shifting shadows of the forest, silver leaves on the interlacing tree branches rustled in the wind. Jack smelled wood smoke. Soon they crossed a sagging footbridge over a stream and came to a clearing with a small stone hut. A fence of woven sticks ringed the yard. Chimney smoke swirled through the afternoon air.

The queen opened the gate, and she and Arthur crossed to the hut. Guinevere knocked on the door.

A moment later, an old woman wrapped in a shawl stood in the doorway. She had a long white braid and luminous skin worn smooth by weather and time, like an ancient stone. The woman's eyes were closed. With a start, Jack realized Cafelle was blind. At her side was a tall white dog with light blue eyes.

Oki didn't bark or whine. The peaceful gaze of the white dog seemed to keep him calm.

"Greetings, Cafelle. We have come to—to seek your help," rasped King Arthur.

Cafelle bowed her head. "Welcome, Your Majesty," she said. "And the queen has come with you this time, yes?"

"Yes, Cafelle." Guinevere touched the blind woman's arm.

"Welcome, dear lady," said Cafelle. "And there are others with you as well. Children?"

"Yes. Jack and Annie," said the queen.

"Annie." The seer reached out, and Annie took her hand. "I see you well, Annie," Cafelle said with her eyes still closed. "You love all animals. You speak your mind and are quick and courageous. Sometimes, though, you move too swiftly. You lack patience."

"That's right, that's me," Annie said with a smile.

"And Jack?" Cafelle said, turning to him.

Jack took the seer's hand.

"You are very thoughtful and intelligent, Jack," she said. "You love books and knowledge. Sometimes, though, you worry too much and you do not act quickly enough."

"Yes, that's me," said Jack.

Oki barked. "And this is our dog, Oki," said Annie. She held out the puppy, and the blind woman patted his head.

"Oki, you are a very happy and lively dog! Very curious and willful," the seer said with a smile. She pointed to the blue-eyed dog at her side. "And this is my Kee. She is old, like me. She cannot hear, and I cannot see. So we must rely on one another."

"Cool," said Annie.

Cafelle then held both her hands out to King Arthur, and he took them in his. "Come inside, my lord," she said. "You have been wounded."

"Yes . . . I have," the king said.

Cafelle and Kee stepped back into the stone hut. The others followed, stepping onto a worn wooden floor.

Inside, Jack could barely see anything. There were no windows and no lanterns. After Cafelle closed the door, the fire from the hearth and two candles were all that illuminated the one-room hut. Once Jack got used to the dim light, he was amazed at how easily Cafelle moved about with Kee at her side. The blind woman pulled a wooden bench close to the hearth, added kindling and logs to the fire, and poked it with a stick until flames shot into the air.

"Pray, sit down," Cafelle said, turning back to her visitors.

Jack and Annie joined Arthur and Guinevere

on the bench, and Cafelle sat on a low stool near the blazing fire. Kee sat beside her.

"Tell me, what do you seek to know, my lord?" Cafelle asked King Arthur.

The king leaned forward into the half circle of firelight. "The ninth dragon ... was stolen ... from Morgan's garden," he said.

"Oh," Cafelle said. "I understand. You need the ninth dragon, my lord, to cross to Avalon."

"I do indeed, wise friend," he said.

Cafelle nodded. Without another word, she stood up and opened the door. Kee joined her at the threshold, and the two stood together, facing the woods outside. Kee's silky white fur glistened in the silver light as the dog looked deep into the forest.

"Write down what she says," Annie whispered.

Jack reached under his cloak and took off his backpack. He pulled out his pencil and notebook and opened to a blank page, ready to write down the seer's prophecy.

Kee joined her at the threshold....

For a long moment, all was quiet except for the gentle rustling of the trees. Gradually, though, the sounds of leaves and wind grew louder and louder until it seemed as if all the forest was shouting its secrets to the blind woman.

Then the force of the wind lessened . . . the whispering and rustling grew softer and softer . . . until a hush fell over the forest.

No one moved as they waited for Cafelle to tell them what the leaves had said.

CHAPTER SIX

Riddle of the Forest

Cafelle turned to face the king. She began to speak in a clear voice:

> *"Moon so bright.*
> *Munith Mor night.*
> *Curtain of white.*
> *Hides from sight.*
> *Magic for flight.*
> *Before dawn's light.*
> *Or lose the fight."*

Jack wrote down her words as fast as he could. When Cafelle finished, she and her dog both stood silent and still in the doorway again.

"Thank you, Cafelle," said the king.

The seer turned to him. "What did I say?" she whispered. She seemed to be in a daze.

Jack read Cafelle's riddle aloud: *"Moon so bright. Munith Mor night. Curtain of white. Hides from sight. Magic for flight. Before dawn's light. Or lose the fight."*

"Oh . . . I see . . . ," said Cafelle. She looked troubled.

Jack was troubled, too. What did the last two lines mean?

"Munith Mor is the highest mountain in the west," said Guinevere. "It seems we should go there first?"

"Yes," said Cafelle. "'Tis not far from the sea. You can see it from the cart path. Continue on your way and journey over the moorlands."

"Good," said Guinevere. "Jack and Annie, you will decipher the rest of the riddle as we travel."

The queen stood and helped the king rise. Jack and Annie and Oki stood up, too. "We must leave at once, Cafelle," said Guinevere. "Not only must we travel to Munith Mor to look for the gold dragon, but we must then take it back to the castle garden in order for its magic to work."

"But, Your Majesty . . . ," said Jack.

"Yes, Jack?" said the queen.

"The last two lines . . . ," he said. The others looked at him as he read the last two lines again: *"Before dawn's light. Or lose the fight."*

"Ah," the queen said. "That seems to say we will lose the fight if we do not arrive in Avalon before dawn." Guinevere took a deep breath. "So we will do all we need to do by dawn tomorrow—travel to Munith Mor, find the gold dragon, and return it to the castle garden. Thank you for your help, Cafelle." She reached out and took the blind woman's hands.

"My lady, you are trembling," Cafelle said.

"I am fine," said Guinevere. Her voice wavered, but she stood tall.

Is she worried we don't have enough time?
Jack thought.

"Thank you, and farewell," said Guinevere.
Then she helped the king toward the door. "Come,
Jack and Annie."

"Thank you, Cafelle," said Annie.

Jack put away his notebook and picked up his
backpack. Then he, Annie, and Oki followed the
king and queen outside into the cool, windy air.
Arthur held on to Guinevere's arm as they walked
away from the stone hut and through the gate. Oki
scampered ahead of them, yapping at windblown
leaves.

Jack glanced back at Cafelle and Kee standing
in the doorway of the hut. The dog could not hear
and the woman could not see, but together the pair
seemed to hear and see more than others could,
Jack thought. He raised his hand in farewell, and
Kee whined *good-bye*.

"Wait! Children!" called Cafelle.

Jack and Annie hurried back to her. The seer
reached into the pocket of her dress. "Take this,"

she said, and she handed them each a small red stone.

"What is it?" asked Jack.

"Rocks from the mountains of fire before time," said the blind woman.

"Lava rocks? Like from volcanoes?" Jack wondered aloud. He rubbed his fingers over his stone. "What do we do with them?"

"Use them to save the king," said the blind woman.

"Use them *how*?" asked Jack.

"With hope and courage," said Cafelle.

"And . . . ?" said Jack.

"With imagination," said the seer.

"Got it! Thanks!" said Annie.

Jack didn't understand. "But what do we do with—"

"Annie? Jack?" Guinevere called from the forest.

"Coming, Your Majesty!" Annie called back.

"Please hurry!" the queen called.

"Go now," said Cafelle.

"Use them to save the king,"
said the blind woman.

"We have to go, Jack!" said Annie. She grabbed him and pulled him away. "Bye! Thank you, Cafelle! Thanks, Kee!" she called back to them. "Thanks for everything!"

"But I don't understand," Jack said to Annie. "What do we do with these stones?"

"Use our imaginations!" said Annie.

"But *how*, exactly?" said Jack.

"Don't worry! We'll figure it out. We have to hurry! Come on!" said Annie. And she took off running through the forest.

Jack looked back at the hut. Cafelle and Kee had gone inside.

"Hurry, Jack!" called Annie.

"Darn," said Jack, annoyed. He crammed his stone into a pocket of his jeans and ran after the others.

Jack caught up with everyone at the footbridge. Annie picked up Oki and carried him across the stream. The queen helped Arthur into the back of the cart. The king trembled as he drank deeply from the leather flask. Again, Jack worried about running out of the healing water.

When he finished drinking, Arthur lay back on the hay and closed his eyes.

"We must hurry," Guinevere said quietly to Jack and Annie, "or all will be lost."

"Yes, Your Majesty," said Jack.

"Keep him warm," Annie whispered to Oki. She put the puppy next to Arthur, and the little dog cuddled against the king again.

"On to Munith Mor," the queen said. Then she hoisted herself into the back of the cart.

Jack and Annie climbed onto the drivers' bench. Annie picked up the reins.

"Hike!" she said.

In the failing light, the yoked oxen began lumbering up the road toward the distant mountain peaks.

"Hurry!" Annie said, shaking the reins.

But the oxen kept their slow pace as the cart creaked and bumped over the rough ground. *How will we ever make it to the mountain, find the gold dragon, and return to the castle before dawn?* Jack wondered. *And what does Cafelle expect us to do with the red stones?*

"We need more information," he said to Annie. "We should have learned more about the stones."

"We had to hurry," said Annie.

"I know, but you lack patience," said Jack, quoting Cafelle.

"Well, you don't act quickly enough," said Annie. "And you worry too much."

Both of them were silent for a moment.

"Read the riddle again," said Annie.

Jack pulled out his notebook and read: *"Moon so bright."* He stopped.

"Keep going," said Annie.

Jack read the next line: *"Munith Mor night."* He paused again.

"Keep going, keep going!" said Annie.

"No! Let's discuss each line," said Jack.

"But we know what *those* lines mean," said Annie. "Plus we need to think about the whole riddle."

"The way to figure out the whole riddle is piece by piece, line by line," said Jack. He looked back at his notebook. *"Moon so—"*

Jack's reading was interrupted by a gasp from Annie. He looked up. "What?"

"Wolf pack!" she whispered.

In the distance, three horsemen in black cloaks were riding across a burnt field, heading toward the road.

"Oh, man." Jack's hands shook as he stuffed his notebook into his pack. He looked back at the queen. "Invaders ahead!" he said.

Guinevere nodded and covered the king's face with his ragged cloak. Then she slumped down in the hay beside him and tucked her golden hair under the hood of her own cloak.

Jack could barely breathe as he and Annie watched the riders leave the field and start galloping down the road toward them.

CHAPTER SEVEN

Run for Your Lives!

Oki barked furiously at the three men on horse-back.

"Oki! Quiet!" Jack commanded.

"Tell them your sister and your parents have a disease," said Annie.

"What?" said Jack. He could barely hear Annie above Oki's barks. "Quiet!" he said. But the puppy kept barking.

"I have a *terrible disease*, Jack," Annie said. "Here, take the reins." She pushed them into

Jack's hands. Then she grabbed his backpack and started digging through it.

"What are you doing?" he asked.

"I have a disease," Annie said, keeping her head down.

"What do you mean?" said Jack.

Annie said something, but Jack couldn't hear her.

Oki barked louder as the riders galloped closer and closer. As they pulled up in front of the cart, Jack saw that the men had grimy faces, bristly beards, and knotted hair down to their shoulders.

"Halt!" the biggest man ordered.

Jack pulled on the reins to stop the oxen. Oki barked and growled from the cart.

"Quiet!" Jack ordered the puppy. He was gripping the reins so tightly his knuckles were white.

The huge rider glared at him with small, mean eyes. "Who are you?" he snarled.

Oki barked and growled from the cart.

"I'm Jack and she's my sister, Annie," said Jack. He tried to keep his voice steady.

Annie didn't look up. She was still hunched over the backpack. Jack had no idea what she was doing.

The rider glanced toward the back of the cart. "Who lies there?" he asked.

"Tell them about our *disease*," Annie said, keeping her head down.

"Um . . . our mother and father . . . they're sick," said Jack. "And my sister—she's sick, too."

"Bad disease!" hissed Annie.

"They all have a bad disease!" Jack had to shout to be heard above Oki's barking.

"What disease?" growled the rider.

"I'm sorry, what?" said Jack.

"What is their bad disease?" the man said.

"Well, it, uh . . . it's—" Jack stammered.

"Yellow fever!" Annie shouted. She threw off her hood and looked up at the men. "Run for your lives!"

Jack nearly fell off the cart. Annie looked terrible! Her face was covered with bright yellow spots!

The men pulled back. Grunting and growling,

they spurred their horses past the cart. The horses broke into a gallop, and the thieves thundered away.

"Well, how rude was that?" said Annie, laughing.

"What happened to you?" cried Jack, staring at her.

Annie held up the yellow marker from Jack's backpack, the one he'd used to highlight the puppy book.

Jack burst out laughing, too. "Oh, man, that was quick thinking."

"Thank you!" said Annie.

Jack looked back at the king and queen. Arthur had slept through the whole incident. Guinevere was sitting up, holding Oki. The puppy was still barking at the fleeing horsemen.

"What happened?" the queen asked. "Oki was barking so loudly, I could not hear. Where did those men go?"

"Annie saved us, Your Majesty," said Jack. "She tricked them. I don't think we'll be seeing them again."

"What did you do, Annie?" said the queen.

Annie turned around and grinned. Guinevere cried out in alarm.

"It's okay!" said Annie, laughing. "I just marked my face with this!" She held up Jack's highlighter. "I told them we all had yellow fever."

"Oh. Oh!" said Guinevere. "I see!" Then she started to laugh, too.

"All right! Let's get this show back on the road!" said Jack. Their success had lifted his spirits. He shook the reins. "Hike!"

The oxen started forward, and the queen settled back in the cart. Jack pulled his notebook out of his pack and handed it to Annie. "Read the riddle again," he said. "We'll figure it out."

Annie read aloud: *Moon so bright. Munith Mor night. Curtain of white.*

Curtain of white, Jack broke in. "That's probably just a white curtain, right? Like a window curtain inside a house?"

"Maybe," said Annie. "Or a curtain in front of a closet?"

"Maybe," said Jack. "Keep reading."

Annie read more: *"Hides from sight."*

"Wait," said Jack. "Does that mean the *curtain* hides from sight? So it's a hidden curtain?"

"Maybe," said Annie. "Or maybe . . . the curtain is hiding something else?"

"Yes!" said Jack. "That makes more sense. Keep reading."

Annie read on: *"Magic for flight.* Do you think *magic for flight* is what the curtain is hiding?"

"Yes!" said Jack again. "I'll bet the robbers hid the gold dragon behind a white curtain."

"That's it!" said Annie.

"But I wonder where they are," said Jack.

"Who? The robbers?" asked Annie.

"Yeah," said Jack. "What if we run into them when we find the place with the curtain?"

"Well, we could try the yellow marker trick again," said Annie.

"But if it's nighttime?" said Jack.

"Hmm, maybe not," said Annie. "Let's just find the white curtain first."

"Okay," said Jack. "Read the last lines."

Annie read aloud: *"Before dawn's light. Or lose the fight."*

"That means we have to hurry," said Jack.

"Yep," said Annie. "Hurry."

Dark clouds covered the sky as the cart creaked and rattled over the weedy path. The air was heavy with impending rain. Jack glanced back at the king and queen. The king was shivering as Guinevere wiped his forehead with a cloth.

The queen looked up and caught Jack's gaze. "He is very weak now," she said. "But he never gives up. No matter how great the struggle, he and his knights never give up. They keep going, without food and rest, through wind and hail and freezing cold."

"We do that, too," said Annie.

"We never give up," said Jack, sitting a little straighter.

"Thank you, Jack and Annie," said Guinevere.

The oxen pulled the cart past deserted farms, thatched huts, and clusters of orchards. As they traveled farther across the countryside, there were fewer and fewer trees. Just before sunset, they came to an open plain that stretched from the base of a mountain. There was no road or path to follow.

"Your Majesty, could this be the moorlands at the foot of Munith Mor that Cafelle talked about?" asked Annie.

"Yes, it could be," said Guinevere.

"So we keep going," said Jack. "Hike!"

The oxen started across the moorlands. Riding over the scrubby land toward the mountains, Jack searched for any sign of a human settlement. He looked in vain for a hut, a fort, a tent, a lighted window, or chimney smoke. *Where will we ever find a white curtain?* he wondered.

As the sky darkened to dusk, the wind blew harder and a thin drizzle started to fall. Jack pulled off his cloak and held it out to the queen. "Your Majesty, please give this to King Arthur," he said.

"Thank you." Guinevere took Jack's cloak and

covered the sleeping king and Oki. Annie pulled her cloak off, too. "And for *you*, Your Majesty," she said.

"No, Annie, you must keep yourself warm," said Guinevere.

"Please take it," said Annie. "I'm fine. Really."

The queen took the cloak and wrapped it around her shoulders.

"You children are very kind," she said.

"No problem," said Jack, though he was freezing. The drizzle had quickly become a windblown rain.

"Your Majesty, can you tell us about the Isle of Avalon?" asked Annie.

"I have never been there, Annie," said Guinevere. "But Arthur has. He tells me it is a large island in a vast, hidden lake surrounded by mountains. It is covered with green pastures and groves of apple trees."

"Apple trees?" said Jack, shivering in the gloomy rain.

"In truth, *Avalon* means 'apples,'" said the queen. "But the isle has trees of all kinds, as well as flowers, birds, butterflies, and animals, both magical and real."

Oki barked. "Yes, like *you*," the queen said, smiling at the puppy. "Arthur says that swans pull boats and mermaids swim in the lake."

"Mermaids!" exclaimed Annie. "Really?"

"Yes, and Avalon has sunshine and gentle breezes and clear, starry nights all year long, and the air smells of lilac and lavender," said the queen. As she spoke, her words seemed to soothe the elements: the rain clouds passed, the wind died down, and the air grew warmer. The nearly full moon was rising over the moorlands, shining brightly in the early-evening sky.

"Sounds like heaven," said Jack.

"Our most beautiful dreams and happiest thoughts come from Avalon," said Guinevere. "There is singing and poetry and playacting, dancing and games and running and swimming. I remember when Arthur journeyed there once with Merlin. He—"

The queen's story was interrupted by a sudden jolt. The cart jerked forward violently, and Jack and Annie were thrown from the bench onto the wet grass.

CHAPTER EIGHT
Munith Mor

The oxen bellowed. Oki barked wildly.

"Jack! Annie!" Guinevere cried. As she climbed out of the back of the cart, Oki was barking, but King Arthur slept on. "Are you all right?"

"Yes, Your Majesty," Annie said, standing up with Jack.

"The rope snapped in two," said Jack.

"I see," said the queen. The wooden pole that had been lashed to the oxen's yoke had fallen to the ground. The rope was frayed and broken. The oxen were no longer connected to the cart.

"Can we fix it?" Annie asked hopefully.

"No, I fear not," the queen said, holding the pieces of the rope. She took a deep breath. "Nothing can be fixed now. Even if we get to Munith Mor and find the gold dragon statue, we will never get back to Camelot's garden by dawn."

"Oh," said Annie.

No one said anything for a moment.

Finally Jack broke the silence. "We never give up," he said. "We have to do something."

"Like what?" said Annie.

"We'll have to walk," said Jack.

"The king cannot walk, Jack," said the queen. "He is too weak."

"Then we'll pull him in the cart," said Jack. "The pole is still attached. Annie and I can pick it up and pull the cart to Munith Mor."

"Sure," said Annie. "It's not that far. We're almost there. We can do it."

Guinevere took a deep breath. "Yes," she said. "Thank you, children. I will pull, too."

"Should we take the yoke off the oxen first?"

Annie asked. "Maybe they'll return home on their own."

"Yes, of course," said the queen.

With Guinevere's help, Jack and Annie lifted the heavy yoke from the necks of the two oxen and set it on the ground.

"Go home. You're free," Jack said.

Neither ox moved.

"Go back home to Camelot," said Annie. "That's what we need you to do now. Don't worry about us."

The heavy animals snorted. Then they both began lumbering back across the moor.

"Good job! Bye, guys! Thanks!" Annie called after them.

"Come on, let's get going," said Jack. He picked up his pack. As he placed it in the back of the cart, he saw that the king was still sleeping in the hay under his cloak. Oki was lying on the king's chest. "Good dog. Stay with him," Jack whispered.

Jack hurried to Annie and Guinevere. "Ready?" he said.

"Ready," they both answered.

Jack and Annie stood at one end of the pole, and Guinevere stood at the other. "Okay, team!" said Jack. "Grab and lift!"

All of them wrapped their arms around the wooden pole. "Heave!" said Annie. Puffing and panting, they lifted the pole off the ground.

"Onward!" said Jack. Gripping the pole, they struggled together, trying to move the cart forward. But it didn't budge.

"Wait, I'll push," said Jack. He went to the back of the cart and pushed. He pushed so hard that his feet slipped, and he fell to his knees. But he scrambled up and tried again.

As Jack pushed, Annie and Guinevere pulled from the front. The cart rocked forward, then slipped back. Jack pushed as hard as he could. Finally the wheels creaked and moaned, and the cart began rolling over the ground.

"Yay! Keep going," called Annie.

Keep going echoed in Jack's mind as he pushed the cart across the moor. Even the squeak of the wheels seemed to say *Keep going, keep going.*

Jack kept pushing while Annie and Guinevere kept pulling, until at last the cart rolled to a stop at the foot of the mountains.

"We're here," Jack said, panting. He ran to the front of the cart and helped Annie and Guinevere lower the pole to the ground.

Then they all looked up at Munith Mor looming overhead.

A stream of moonlit water splashed over the ridges of the mountainside. The shimmering white waterfall spilled into a pool and then coursed down a narrow streambed. Except for the soft rushing sound of the water, the night was still.

"Are we in Avalon?" a deep voice rasped. King Arthur was sitting up in the hay.

The queen hurried to him. "We are very close," she said.

"Help . . . help me down," he said.

As Guinevere helped Arthur from the back of the cart, Annie put Oki on the ground. Then she turned to Jack. "We have to solve Cafelle's riddle now," she said.

Jack kept pushing while Annie
and Guinevere kept pulling.

Jack pulled his notebook out of his backpack and turned to the riddle. "There's not enough light," he said.

"Don't worry, we can remember," said Annie. *"Moon so bright. Munith Mor night."*

"Then *Curtain of white. Hides from sight,"* said Jack.

"Yes! *Magic for flight,"* said Annie.

"Got it," said Jack. He repeated the whole riddle: *"Moon so bright. Munith Mor night. Curtain of white. Hides from sight. Magic for flight. Before dawn's light. Or lose the fight."*

"The moon is bright, and we're at Munith Mor," said Annie. "So where's the curtain?"

They looked around at the barren landscape.

"That's the big question," said Jack.

"Hey, look at that waterfall!" said Annie. "Doesn't it kind of look like a curtain?"

Jack stared at the sparkling torrent flowing over the side of the mountain. It *did* look like a curtain, he thought.

"Yes! A *curtain of white!"* Jack said.

"Hides from sight!" said Annie. "The water-fall's hiding something!"

"Magic for flight," said Jack.

"The gold dragon statue!" said Annie.

"Behind the waterfall!" said Jack.

"That's the hidden place!" said Annie.

"Yes!" said Jack. He turned to the king and queen. "The gold dragon is somewhere behind that waterfall," he said.

"We're going to check it out. You guys stay here," Annie said to the queen. "I mean, *Your Majesties* stay here."

Guinevere smiled. "Pray, be careful," she said.

"We will," said Annie. As she and Jack started toward the waterfall, Oki ran along beside them.

"No! Go back!" Jack commanded.

Oki barked at him.

"Let's just put him in your bag," said Annie. She picked up the puppy and lowered him into Jack's backpack. "There you go."

"Come on!" said Jack. And they headed toward the shimmering curtain of white.

"Wait, I need to wash off the yellow marks!" said Annie. She ran to the streambed and splashed water on her face. When she finished, she hurried back to Jack. "All set," she said.

Jack and Annie climbed up to a rocky ledge and gazed at the cascade. Oki sneezed in Jack's pack. "Hang in there, buddy," said Jack. "Okay. See that rock formation jutting out? See how the water shoots over it and then splashes down on the rocks below? It looks like there's an opening of some kind behind the waterfall . . . doesn't it?"

"Yes!" Annie said. "Let's go!"

CHAPTER NINE
Fire Dragon

Jack followed Annie over the wet rocks to the waterfall. In the moonlight, he could barely make out a hollow space in the cliff behind it.

"That looks like a cave!" said Annie.

"A cave that *hides from sight* behind a *curtain of white*," said Jack.

Yip! Yip! Oki popped his head out of Jack's backpack.

The little dog kept barking as Jack and Annie slipped behind the waterfall and made their way inside the cave.

Okay. See that rock formation jutting out?

The air in the cramped cave smelled of wet rocks and mold. Jack had to bend down to keep his head from hitting the ceiling, and Oki tumbled out of his backpack.

Before Jack could catch him, the puppy dashed off.

"Oki!" cried Annie.

Yip! Yip!

Oki's barking came from deep within the cave. "We're coming!" called Annie. She and Jack moved their hands along the cave wall to guide their way. As they followed the sound of Oki's barks and whines, the cave became more like a tunnel. The ceiling was so low that Annie and Jack had to get on their hands and knees and crawl in the blackness toward Oki's cries.

Suddenly Jack heard a flapping and squeaking off to the side. "Watch out for bats," he called.

"Yikes. You think spiders could be in here, too?" said Annie.

"Probably yes," said Jack.

"Oh, no," said Annie.

"Keep going," said Jack. "Just keep your head down."

Close by, Oki yelped furiously.

Jack felt around blindly for the puppy. But instead of fur, his hand touched a cold, smooth object. He quickly drew back, afraid he might have touched a snake or some other creature.

"Gotcha!" said Annie. "I got Oki!"

"Good," said Jack.

"Hey, there's something else here," said Annie.

"What?" said Jack.

"It's heavy, but it feels like a plate," said Annie.

"Actually, I felt something, too," said Jack. He reached out and touched the cold object again. He picked it up and ran his fingers over it. "I think I found a goblet," he said.

"I just found something else," said Annie. "Oh, wow . . . it's too heavy to lift with one hand."

"Where is it?" said Jack, reaching toward the sound of Annie's voice.

"Here," said Annie. She guided his hand to the object.

When Jack tried to pick the object up, he almost dropped it. It was *very* heavy. Jack ran his fingers over its surface. . . . *Is that a head? A snout?* he wondered. *Wings? Claws?* "Oh, man, we found it!" he whispered.

"The dragon?" asked Annie.

"Yes, I think so!" said Jack. "Let's get it outside!"

"Okay, I'll carry Oki," said Annie.

Jack stuffed the heavy object in his backpack. Crawling and then crouching, he and Annie made their way back through the cave, until they came to the entrance. The waterfall showered them with spray as they climbed over the rocks to the ground.

Jack set down his backpack and pulled out the object. In the moonlight, the ninth dragon was magnificent. Its golden wings were raised behind its back, and its eyes seemed to be gazing into the far distant hills.

"Your Majesties!" Annie called. "We found the ninth dragon!" She put Oki on the ground, and they all hurried to show Arthur and Guinevere the golden statue. But when they reached the cart, there was no sign of the king or queen.

"Where are they?" said Jack.

Oki yelped and dashed into the shadows.

"There they are!" said Annie, pointing to a cluster of rocks.

Guinevere was kneeling on the grass, holding Arthur in her arms. Oki whined and pawed the ground.

"We found it!" Jack shouted as he and Annie ran to them.

Jack placed the gold dragon statue next to Arthur. "See, we found the ninth dragon!" he said. But Arthur and Guinevere were both still.

"What—what's wrong?" said Annie.

"The king is dying," the queen said in a hollow voice.

Oki let out a howl.

"He can't be," said Jack. Not *now.* "What about the water, the healing water from Avalon? Wait!"

Jack ran to the cart and grabbed the leather flask and brought it back to the queen.

"There is no more," said Guinevere.

Jack turned the leather flask upside down. Not a drop of the healing water was left.

"Listen," said Annie.

Jack heard a faint whinnying sound and the thunder of horse hooves. Peering across the moonlit moor, he saw riders in the distance galloping toward them.

"The robbers," said Guinevere.

"Oh, no," said Annie.

"They're coming back for their treasure," said the queen.

Jack started to tremble. The king was dying. The enemy was coming.

"There is no hope," Guinevere said softly.

Jack took a deep breath. "Yes, there is," he said. "There's hope."

"There is?" said Annie.

"Yes. We can save the king," said Jack.

"We can?" said Annie.

"Yes. We have to keep going," said Jack.

The thundering of the horses' hooves grew louder.

"Keep going? How?" said Annie.

"We just have to keep going," said Jack. "We have to do the next right thing."

"But what's that? What's the next right thing?" said Annie.

"I don't know!" said Jack.

"Wait a minute," said Annie. "I just remembered! Our stones from Cafelle!"

"Yes!" said Jack. He and Annie reached into their pockets and pulled out the red stones. "But what do we do with them?" Jack said.

"We use them with hope and strength! And imagination!" said Annie. "That's what Cafelle told us to do!"

Jack clasped his stone. He stared at the dragon statue and tried to feel hopeful and strong and use his imagination. "Long live King Arthur and Queen Guinevere!" he said.

"Long live goodness! And kindness!" said Annie.

"And courage!" said Jack.

"And patience!" said Annie.

"And never giving up!" said Jack.

As Jack and Annie shouted their words, the gold dragon began to glow as if it were lit from within. It glowed brighter and brighter and grew warmer and warmer. The statue glowed so brightly that it looked like it was on fire.

"Long live Camelot!" said Jack. "And Morgan's library and all the books!"

"Long live the castle gardens and flowers!" said Annie. "And the Great Hall! And music!"

"Long live myths and legends!" shouted Jack. "From *all* times and places!"

Jack heard thunder, but it wasn't the thunder of horse hooves. Jack felt trembling, but it wasn't the trembling of his body. The rumbling and quaking came from the statue. The very air around the gold dragon quivered.

"Long live Morgan and Merlin and Teddy and Kathleen!" shouted Jack.

"And all the knights and ladies and children

and horses and oxen of Camelot!" said Annie.

"Long live Annie!" said Jack.

"Long live Jack!" shouted Annie. "And Oki!"

Hissing, cracking, screaming sounds rocked the night. A mighty explosion and a great blast shook the earth. With a thunderous roll, a billowing cloud erupted from the top of Munith Mor. The cloud burst into flame, and with a deafening roar, a gigantic fire-red dragon rose from the flames and seemed to spread its wings over the world.

CHAPTER TEN

All Good

The dragon's eyes were flaming. Its horns and claws and scaly skin flashed in the moonlight. Its open batlike wings began moving against the night sky, sweeping back and forth, back and forth. Jack, Annie, Oki, and Guinevere huddled with the king in the raging windstorm. In a flash of fire and smoke, a portal opened before them. Colors swirled—red, black, yellow, and green. Images from mythic realms of the otherworld passed by Jack's eyes. Flying stags, gossamer-winged fairies, one-eyed ice wizards, spider queens, raven kings, water horses, wolf shadows, sea serpents, snow giants, and fallen knights all flew by, ghostly and real at the same time. And then nothing. Nothing at all. Only darkness.

Annie's voice broke through the black silence. "Jack. Jack," she said.

Jack opened his eyes. He was sitting in soft wet grass, still clasping the red stone Cafelle had given him. Annie sat beside him, and Guinevere and Arthur lay nearby.

Jack heard water splashing. It sounded as if fish were jumping, but when he sat up, he couldn't see anything through a golden mist that was rising from a lake. The breeze was soft and smelled of lavender and lilac. "What happened?" he said.

"We were pulled into the portal, and it brought us to Avalon," said Annie.

Yip! Oki popped up beside her.

"Right, Oki?" Annie asked.

"I believe you are right," answered the queen.

Jack and Annie turned around. Guinevere was sitting up, her golden hair tumbling around her shoulders. She looked dazed but happy. "How are you both?" she said.

"I think we're good," said Annie.

"All good," said Jack. He slipped the red stone back into his pocket.

Guinevere smiled at them. Then she reached out and tenderly touched the king's shoulder. "Wake, my lord," she said.

King Arthur opened his eyes and stared up at the pale sky. Oki scampered over the grass and licked the king's cheek. Arthur laughed softly and stroked the puppy's fur.

"Where's the dragon?" said Jack.

"You're sitting beside him," said Annie.

Jack looked down and saw the gold statue shining in the dewy grass. When he wrapped his hand around it, the statue was still warm. "What about the giant living, breathing dragon?" he asked.

"I don't know," said Annie.

"Everyone saw a giant dragon, right?" said Jack. "It wasn't just me?"

"Yes, I saw it," said Guinevere.

"And I," said the king, sitting up. Arthur's voice was hoarse, but his eyes were clear. Color had returned to his face.

"Oh, wow, Your Majesty! Are you going to be okay now?" asked Annie.

The king took a deep breath. "Yes, Annie. I believe my wound has already begun to heal."

"I'm really glad," Annie said.

"Me too," said Jack.

Suddenly Oki let out a yelp. Then the puppy dashed to the shore of the lake and barked wildly. High, beautiful singing was coming from across the mist-covered water.

"Who's singing?" Jack asked.

"Mermaids," said the king.

"Mermaids?" said Annie.

Jack just smiled. In this strange new world, nothing seemed impossible.

"Look!" said Annie.

Slowly, a cinnamon-colored boat with a white

sail glided out of the haze. At the helm of the boat was a tall bearded man in a blue robe. A small penguin stood beside him.

"Merlin! Penny!" breathed Annie. She and Jack jumped up and ran to the edge of the water.

When Merlin saw Jack and Annie, his eyes grew wide with astonishment.

Peep, chirped Penny.

"Greetings!" called Jack.

"Greetings, indeed!" said the magician. "How on earth do you children come to be here in Avalon?"

"Magic!" said Annie.

Merlin landed the small sailboat, and he and Penny came ashore. Oki rushed forward and nuzzled the baby penguin's fuzzy head. Penny flapped her wings and made squeaking sounds as if she was giggling.

"New friends!" Guinevere said.

Merlin cried out in amazement when he saw the king and queen walking toward him. "Your Majesties!" said the magician. "What has happened? Why are you all here in Avalon?"

"Soon after you left Camelot, word came of enemy forces in the east," said the king. As he began telling Merlin the story of the invaders, a snow-white unicorn pranced out of the golden haze. Teddy and Kathleen were on its back.

"Dianthus!" Annie cried. "Teddy! Kathleen!"

"Hi!" yelled Jack, and he and Annie ran away from the shore to greet their friends.

Teddy and Kathleen shouted with wonder and joy when they saw Jack and Annie. The young enchanters jumped off the unicorn and threw their arms around them. Oki yapped and leapt joyfully around Dianthus.

"Hi, Dianthus! We missed you!" said Annie. She lifted Oki up to the unicorn. Dianthus sniffed the puppy, and Oki licked him.

"Why have you come here?" asked Kathleen.

"King Arthur was wounded," said Jack.

"Wounded? Badly?" Teddy asked.

"Yes, but he's better now," said Jack. "See?" They looked back at the king and queen, who were talking with Merlin near the lake.

"And we hope Morgan can make him even better," said Annie. "That's why we came here."

"Where *is* Morgan?" asked Jack.

Teddy peered into the mist. "She's . . . there!" he said, pointing toward the water.

Morgan le Fay was emerging from the mist in a small boat pulled by a flock of swans.

"Morgan, look who's here!" called Teddy.

Jack and Annie waved at the enchantress. "Hi, Morgan!" Annie called.

Morgan looked bewildered to see them. Her swan boat glided to the sandy beach, and she stepped ashore. "How? Why?" she said.

Carrying Oki in her arms, Annie ran to Morgan. Jack followed. They told her the whole story, from Oki finding the tree house in the Frog Creek woods to coming to Avalon through the dragon's portal.

"Astonishing," said Morgan when they finished. "And the king and queen are here, too?"

"Yes! There!" Annie pointed farther down

the shore, where Merlin was still talking with the royal couple.

Morgan crossed to King Arthur. "Welcome back to the Isle of Avalon, Your Majesty," she said.

The king smiled and nodded. The enchantress gazed at him for a long moment, then put her hand on his chest and closed her eyes. Finally she smiled and looked at him again. "You will soon be completely healed," she said. "But you and the queen must remain here for a short while, until you are restored to your strongest self."

"Thank you, Morgan," said Guinevere. "And Jack and Annie? May they stay in Avalon with us?"

"I fear they must return to Camelot," said Merlin, stepping forward. "Tonight will be the last night of the full moon. Before the sun rises on Camelot tomorrow, they must restore the gold dragon to its rightful place in the garden, or its power will be lost forever."

"But the dragon is not in its place now," said Teddy. "So how can *they* return, if *we* cannot?"

"*I fear they must return to Camelot,*" said Merlin.

"I imagine they will return in the same fashion that they have traveled here," said Morgan. "With their own special magic."

"Oh!" said Jack. He felt in his pocket for the piece of volcanic rock. "With Cafelle's stones?"

Morgan smiled and nodded. "Yes. I am certain that the magic stones, along with your words of strength and hope, will again call forth the dragon's power to open the portal. When I see Cafelle in Camelot, I will tell her of your courage."

"And I will tell her that you saved my life," King Arthur said.

"We shall be grateful to you both forever," said Queen Guinevere.

"Please tell my knights I will return soon," said King Arthur, "and together we will restore the kingdom."

"Yes, Your Majesty," said Jack.

"It is time," said Merlin.

Everyone grew quiet. Annie and Jack took the red stones from their pockets. Annie held Oki, and Jack picked up the heavy statue of the ninth dragon. Then, with all his heart and all his good feelings for their friends, Jack whispered, "Long live Camelot."

"Long live Camelot," echoed Annie.

Grasping their stones, Jack and Annie whispered these words over and over with hope and strength, until the air crackled and a rushing wind bent the trees. Clouds billowed and spun into swirling white masses, then changed their colors from white to pink to red. And then from the churning crimson sky, the ninth dragon took shape and spread its great wings. In a rush of air and burst of light, Jack and Annie and Oki were lifted off the Isle of Avalon and returned to the castle of Camelot.

CHAPTER ELEVEN
Back to the Garden

Yip? said Oki.

"Wow," said Annie.

"Yes," said Jack. In the first light of dawn, he could see the tangles of vines and flowers, the fishpond, and the stone wall. They were back in Morgan le Fay's secret garden.

Oki leapt from Annie's arms and scurried among the patches of ivy, wild grasses, and shrubs, yapping and yipping at the dragons made of glass and granite, marble, clay, bronze, silver, and seashells.

"The ninth dragon goes behind those yellow rosebushes," said Annie.

"Right," said Jack. "And let's leave Cafelle's magic stones there, too."

Jack carefully placed the statue between the bushes and stone wall. Then he and Annie set Cafelle's stones at its feet. The dragon glistened and shone as it caught the light of the rising sun.

"Good-bye," Jack whispered.

"Long live Camelot," said Annie.

Yip! said Oki.

"Let's go," said Jack. And the three of them left Morgan's garden. They walked through the library and down the musty hallway, down the steep steps and through the rocky passage to the outer courtyard.

Sir Lamorak and Sir Tristan were standing by the entrance gate.

"Hello, sirs!" Annie called from behind them.

The knights whirled around. When they saw Jack and Annie, they lowered their lances.

The dragon glistened and shone as it
caught the light of the rising sun.

"How—how did you get inside?" stammered Sir Lamorak.

"Where are the king and queen?" said Sir Tristan.

"They're safe in Avalon!" said Jack.

"What happened?" said Sir Lamorak.

"It's a long story," said Annie. "But just know that the king will be completely well soon. And when he is, he and Guinevere will come back to the castle."

"And the king said to tell you that he'll work with his knights and all his subjects to restore order to the kingdom," said Jack.

The two knights shook their heads in wonder.

"Bye for now," said Annie. "Hold down the fort!"

Jack, Annie, and Oki headed out the castle entrance gate and started through the hay field. They ran over the dry grass, then pushed their way through the tall wheat stalks waving in the wind. From the field, they headed into the shadowy forest, and Oki led the way around the ancient oaks, until they came to the magic tree house.

"Let's go, buddy!" said Jack.

He lifted the puppy and put him into his pack. Then he and Annie headed up the rope ladder. When they climbed into the tree house, Annie grabbed the Pennsylvania book and pointed at a picture of Frog Creek.

"I wish we could go there!" she said.

The wind started to blow.

The tree house started to spin.

It spun faster and faster.

Then everything was still.

Absolutely still.

The day was cloudy and cool. No time had passed in the Frog Creek woods. The wind shook the tree leaves.

Yip! Oki popped his head out of Jack's pack.

"We're home," said Annie.

"Home, sweet home," said Jack. "Right, little buddy."

Yip!

Jack climbed down the rope ladder, and

Annie followed. Then they started through the Frog Creek woods.

"Should we put Oki on the ground?" said Annie.

"Nope. Keep him in the pack," said Jack.

"All the way to the dog park?" asked Annie.

"Dog park? Are you serious?" said Jack. "You still want to go to the dog park? Aren't you worn out?"

"No, not really," said Annie.

"*Really* not really?" said Jack.

"Really not really," said Annie.

"But we did so much today," said Jack.

"Not really," said Annie. "Oki just led us to the magic tree house. And then we took a little journey to Camelot's secret garden, met a blind seer, scared away robbers, hauled a broken cart across a moor, solved a riddle, explored a hidden cave, found a stolen statue, faced a dragon bigger than a mountain, landed on the Isle of Avalon, saw a unicorn, heard some mermaids, and used magic stones to take the gold dragon back to the garden to help the king and queen and our Camelot friends return to the castle." She shrugged. "And then we came home to Frog Creek."

Jack nodded. "Okay. What you're saying is Oki just took us on a little detour on our way to the dog park."

"That's what I'm saying," said Annie. "So, do you want to go there now?"

"Sure, why not?" said Jack as they headed out of the woods. "And let's stop by the pet store."

"Right. You want to buy a toothbrush and toothpaste for Oki's dental care." said Annie.

"I do," said Jack.

"Cool," said Annie. "You know what? I love our ordinary lives."

"Me too," said Jack. "Long live Frog Creek."

Turn the page for a sneak peek at

Magic Tree House Fact Tracker:
Dragons and Mythical Creatures

Unicorns and Mermaids

Tales about mermaids and unicorns have enchanted people for thousands of years.

One of the most loved children's stories is "The Little Mermaid," written by Hans Christian Andersen in 1837.

Unicorns and mermaids are among the most popular mythical creatures. They've been in movies and on television. Pictures of mermaids and unicorns decorate T-shirts, signs, and logos. There are unicorn and mermaid stuffed animals, toys, and books.

The Mermaid of Zennor

In the village of Zennor on the coast of Cornwall, an ancient stone chair sits next to a church.

The chair honors the memory of a beautiful mermaid. She was Morveren, the daughter of the king of the ocean.

Stories say that she came to Zennor long ago when a young man named Mathew Trewella began singing in the church each evening.

When Morveren heard his wonderful voice, she crept out of the sea to listen. She fell in love with Mathew's singing, and with Mathew as well.

Every night Morveren dressed in a beautiful gown made of pearls and coral to hide her body. Then she went to the village and sat by the church to hear Mathew.

One night Morveren sighed sadly. Mathew heard her. He rushed out to find the lovely creature.

Mathew followed the mermaid as she hurried down to the sea. Together, Mathew and Morveren slowly sank beneath the waves in each other's arms. No one ever saw either of them again.

Quetzalcoatl

The Aztec people of Mexico worshipped a mythical serpent god named Quetzalcoatl (KET-sull-koh-ah-tull). It had a snake's body and beautiful green, blue, and red feathers like those of the quetzal bird. Quetzal feathers were on the headdresses of Aztec kings and priests as a symbol of their god.

Aztecs believed that Quetzalcoatl created the universe. He was the god of the wind and the morning star.

Corn was a big part of the Aztec diet. In one story, a huge red ant led Quetzalcoatl to

a mountain covered with grains and corn. Quetzalcoatl took the corn to the other gods. They all agreed that it was a good food, and people have been eating it ever since.

The Sphinx

Four thousand years ago, the ancient Egyptians made a huge statue of a mythical animal called a sphinx. It has the body of a lion and the head of a person. Experts think the sphinx was there to guard the tombs of Egyptian kings.

The ancient Greeks also had myths about the sphinx. In one story, a sphinx struck terror into the hearts of a Greek town called Thebes. The sphinx said that she would kill all the townspeople unless someone answered her riddle.

The riddle was: What animal has four legs in the morning, two at noon, and three in the evening? One man solved it. He said that the answer was a person.

Think about it. Babies crawl on four legs. Adults walk on two legs. And when they get old, they might need a cane, which gives them three legs.

Love learning with Jack and Annie?
Then track the facts with your favorite
brother-and-sister team in these
Magic Tree House® Fact Trackers!

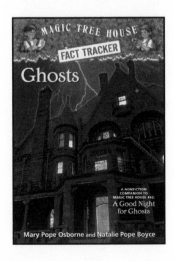

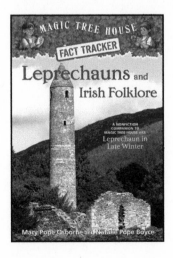